# How 'Bout Them Cowboys!

## Aimee Aryal

### Illustrated by Miguel De Angel

### with M. Cooper, G. Perez, B. Vinson

www.mascotbooks.com

It was a beautiful fall day in Dallas. Rowdy was at Texas Stadium getting ready for a Dallas Cowboys game.

As he walked through the parking lot,
Cowboys fans cheered,
"How 'bout them Cowboys!"

The smell of good food led Rowdy to a Cowboys cookout.

A man behind the grill cheered,
"How 'bout them Cowboys!"

Rowdy stopped at the Cowboys locker room,
where the coach was giving the team
final instructions.

The coach cheered,
"How 'bout them Cowboys!"

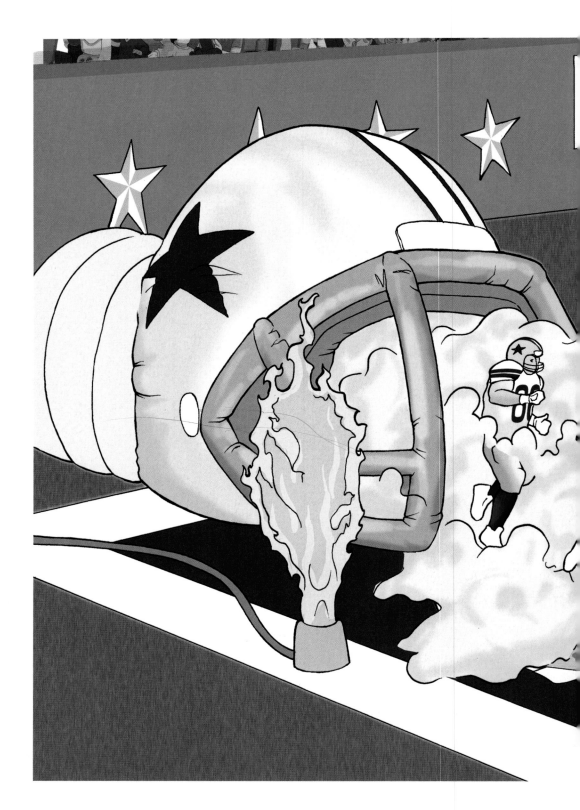

The team entered the stadium wearing their classic Dallas Cowboys uniforms with a blue star on their helmets.

As they ran onto the field, the team cheered, "How 'bout them Cowboys!"

It was now time for Rowdy
to make his entrance.
He rode a four-wheeler onto the field.

He stopped on the star at midfield and cheered, "How 'bout them Cowboys!"

A Cowboys player made a great play
and ran into the end zone.

"Touchdown!" signaled Rowdy.
The coach cheered,
"How 'bout them Cowboys!"

Rowdy entertained Dallas Cowboys fans
during the game and made them laugh.

After seeing Rowdy in action,
Cowboys fans cheered,
"How 'bout them Cowboys!"

Rowdy cheered for "America's Team"
with the world-famous
Dallas Cowboys Cheerleaders.

The cheerleaders cheered,
"How 'bout them Cowboys!"

With the score tied, the Cowboys lined up
for a game winning field goal.

As the ball sailed through the uprights,
the kicker cheered,
"Cowboys win, Rowdy! Cowboys win!"

The Dallas Cowboys won the football game.
The team celebrated and
Rowdy gave the coach a high-five.

Rowdy cheered,
"How 'bout them Cowboys!"

It had been a great day at Texas Stadium.
Rowdy walked home and
went straight to bed.

As Rowdy drifted off to sleep, he thought,
"How 'bout them Cowboys!"

For Anna & Maya - Aimee Aryal

For Sue, Ana Milagros, and Angel Miguel ~ Miguel De Angel

Special Thanks to:

Marjorie Cooper
Gerry Perez
Brad Vinson

# For more information about our products, please visit us online at www.mascotbooks.com.

For more information, please contact Mascot Books,
P.O. Box 220157, Chantilly, VA 20153-0157

ISBN: 1-932888-90-X

Printed in the United States.